Karen's Monsters

Look for these
and other books about Karen
in the
Baby-sitters Little Sister series:

BABY-SITTERS
Little Sister

Karen's Monsters
Ann M. Martin

Illustrations by Susan Tang

A
LITTLE APPLE
PAPERBACK

SCHOLASTIC INC.
New York Toronto London Auckland Sydney

For Laura

No part of this publication may be reproduced in whole or in part, or stored in a retrieval system, or transmitted in any form or by any means, electronic, mechanical, photocopying, recording, or otherwise, without written permission of the publisher. For information regarding permission, write to Scholastic Inc., 555 Broadway, New York, NY 10012.

ISBN 0-590-26279-3

12 11 10 9 8 7 6 5 4 3 2 1   5 6 7 8 9/9 0/0

Printed in the U.S.A.   40

First Scholastic printing, October 1995

Emily Michelle

"Pumpkins are gay on Halloween day," I sang. "But pumpkins are bright on Halloween night."

It was a little early to be singing about Halloween, since it was not even October first yet. But I was thinking about it anyway. I was thinking about it because in school we were working on autumn projects. Autumn made me think about the beginning of the holiday season. And holidays made me think about Halloween.

I just love autumn. I love everything

about it. I love the bright leaves and scare-crows and pumpkins and jack-o'-lanterns and cool nights and the first frost on the ground. And I especially love holidays. Halloween, Thanksgiving, Christmas. My friend Nancy Dawes celebrates Rosh Ha-shanah and Yom Kippur and Hanukkah. Sometimes Nancy and I look in the calendar to see what holidays we might be missing, such as Boxing Day or Summer Bank Hol-iday. We do not even know what they are, but they are interesting to us because they are holidays.

It was the last day of September, which was a Saturday. I was singing while I poked through my school stuff. I was in my bed-room at the little house where I live with my mother, my stepfather Seth, and my little brother Andrew. Andrew is four and I am seven.

My name is Karen. Karen Brewer. I am in second grade at Stoneybrook Academy, in Stoneybrook, Connecticut. My teacher's name is Ms. Colman, and she is so gigundoly wonderful I cannot even believe it. Nancy is in Ms. Colman's class, too. So is Hannie Papadakis. Nancy and Hannie and I are best friends. We call ourselves the Three Musketeers.

I was poking through my school things on a Saturday because the next day Andrew and I would go to my father's house for a month. Our parents are divorced, but they both live in Stoneybrook. So Andrew and I go back and forth — a month at Mommy's house, a month at Daddy's house. Whenever we switch, I have to remember to take my school books and papers and projects with me.

I had made a pile on my bed. "Does that look like everything?" I asked my rat. (I have a pet rat, who lives in a big cage. Andrew has a pet hermit crab. We just love animals.)

Brring rang the telephone. Mommy answered it downstairs. A few seconds later, I heard her call, "Karen! Phone for you! It's David Michael."

David Michael is my stepbrother, who lives at Daddy's house. He is seven. Sometimes we are good friends. Sometimes he is a big fat pest. I wondered what he wanted.

"Hello?" I said, when I picked up the phone.

"Hi, Karen," said David Michael. "I just wanted to tell you something."

"What?"

"Beware of Emily. She has turned into a monster."

"Emily has?" Emily is only two and a half. She is my sister at the big house. I could not imagine Emily as a monster. She is way too little. "What do you mean?" I asked.

"She is always screaming and yelling and kicking now. Yesterday she bit your dad. You better monster-proof yourself before you come over here tomorrow."

"Thank you for the warning," I said politely. But I did not plan to monster-proof myself. For one thing, I did not know how to do that. For another, I just did not think Emily could be so bad. And if she was? Well, I could handle a little monster.

I was still looking forward to going to the big house.

Emily Two-Two

I have special nicknames for my brother and me. I call us Andrew Two-Two and Karen Two-Two. This is because we have two of so many things — two houses and two families, two mommies and two daddies, two cats and dogs. Let me tell you how we became two-twos.

It started a long time ago, when I was just a little kid. Back then I had just one house and one family, one mommy and one daddy. Andrew and I lived with our mommy and daddy in a big house here in

Stoneybrook. It was the house Daddy had grown up in. I thought we were happy, but I guess we were not. At least, Mommy and Daddy were not. They began to fight a little. Then they fought a lot. They fought all the time. Finally they told Andrew and me that they were going to get a divorce. They did not want to live together anymore. They loved Andrew and me very much, but they did not love each other.

So Mommy moved to a little house. Soon she got married again. Daddy stayed in the big house. He got married again, too. And that is how my brother and I wound up with two families.

In my little-house family are Mommy, Seth, Andrew, me, Rocky, Midgie, Emily Junior, and Bob. Rocky and Midgie are Seth's cat and dog. Emily Junior is my rat. Bob is Andrew's hermit crab. Guess what. Emily Junior and Bob are two-twos, too. They go back and forth between the big house and the little house with Andrew and me.

In my big-house family are Daddy, Elizabeth, Andrew, me, Kristy, Sam, Charlie, David Michael, Emily Michelle, Nannie, Shannon, Boo-Boo, Goldfishie, Crystal Light the Second, Emily Junior, and Bob. Isn't it good the big house is so big? Elizabeth is my stepmother. Kristy, Sam, Charlie, and David Michael are her kids. (She was married once before she married Daddy.) Kristy is thirteen. She baby-sits. I love her. I am glad she is my big sister. Sam and Charlie go to high school. Sam is fifteen and Charlie is seventeen. Charlie plays on his school football team. And David Michael is seven, like me. But he does not go to my school. He goes to Stoneybrook Elementary. Emily Michelle is my adopted sister. Daddy and Elizabeth adopted her from the country of Vietnam. I love my little sister, which is why I named my rat after her. Nannie is Elizabeth's mother. That makes her my stepgrandmother. She moved into the big house to help take care of it and all the kids and pets. The pets are Boo-Boo

8

(Daddy's nasty old cat), Shannon (David Michael's puppy), Goldfishie and Crystal Light (Andrew's and my fish), and Emily Junior and Bob.

Now Andrew and I have two of everything (almost). We have clothes and books and toys at each house. I even have my two best friends. Nancy lives next door to Mommy, and Hannie lives across the street from Daddy. (Plus I happen to have two pairs of glasses — a blue pair for reading and a pink pair for the rest of the time.)

Being a two-two might sound confusing, but mostly it is okay. Sometimes when I am at the little house, I miss my big-house family. Sometimes when I am at the big house, I miss my little-house family. But I am very lucky to have two families who love me so much.

"Okay, Emily Two-Two," I said to my rat. "Are you ready to go to Daddy's tomorrow? We will have fun there. And we will find out if Emily Michelle really is a monster."

Autumn

"Karen? Andrew? Are you ready?" called Mommy.

"Yes!" I replied.

Andrew and I hurried down the stairs in the little house. My backpack thumped against me with each step. It was full of my school things, the ones I needed to take to Daddy's.

Mommy and Seth and Andrew and I climbed into our car. Seth drove us to the big house.

"Good-bye," said Andrew and I when Seth had parked the car.

"Good-bye," replied Mommy and Seth.

We gave each other kisses. Then Andrew and I ran across the lawn and into Daddy's house. "We're here!" I cried.

Everyone came running — Daddy, Elizabeth, David Michael, Emily Michelle, Kristy, Nannie, Sam, and Charlie. We all began talking at once.

"Cool! There is Bob. I'll take him, Andrew," said Sam.

"Are you hungry?" asked Nannie.

"Where is Boo-Boo?" asked Andrew.

"I bake cookie!" said Emily proudly.

"She does not look like a monster," I whispered to David Michael.

"Just you wait," he replied.

Andrew and I put our things in our bedrooms. We helped Emily Junior and Bob settle down. Then David Michael said to us, "Come on outside. Everyone is there. We are going to rake leaves today."

I know that raking leaves is supposed to be a big fat chore. But I do not mind it (even though sometimes I pretend to mind). I do not mind it because I like raking the leaves into piles and jumping in the piles. Daddy always lets us do that.

Andrew and I followed David Michael outside. Sure enough, the rest of my big-house family was there. Almost everybody was holding a rake. (Not Emily. She was trying to push her doll stroller around the yard. She was not helping with the leaves, but she certainly did not look like a little monster.)

There were no rakes left, so Andrew played fetch with Shannon. I listened to the big kids talk. Kristy said she was very busy with baby-sitting. Sam was worried about a test he had taken.

"I bet you did fine on the test," Charlie said to him. "Stop worrying. Hey, I know. You can help me with our Halloween float, since you do not have to do anything for the math club's float."

"What Halloween float?" I asked.

"The high school is going to put on a Halloween parade this year," replied Charlie. "It is supposed to get everyone interested in the homecoming football game. Every group or club or team at SHS" (that stands for Stoneybrook High School) "is going to make a float for the parade," Charlie continued. "The football team's float is going to be called Monsters of the Gridiron."

"Of the what?" I said.

"The gridiron. That is another word for football field. Anyway, we are going to make all these monsters for our float — Frankenstein and Dracula, even Bigfoot. I am in charge of Frankenstein. Anybody who wants to help me build him is welcome."

"Cool," I said. "What — "

"Karen! Hey, Karen! You got here!"

I saw Hannie running across the street with her brother Linny and her little sister

14

Sari. They wanted to play in our leaf piles. So that is what we did.

Emily played with us, too. She did not do one monsterish thing.

I told David Michael he was crazy.

The Little Monster

I can get ready for school very fast. This is because I usually choose my clothes the night before. Then I lay them out on a chair. When I wake up the next morning, I do not have to think about what to wear. I just roll out of bed and put those clothes on.

That is what I did when I woke up in my room at the big house the next day. I put on my yellow plaid skirt, red turtleneck, red tights, and my black slip-on shoes. Then I ran to the bathroom. If I hurried, I could be the first person to sit down at the

16

breakfast table. But I could not get into the bathroom. Somebody else was already in it. Boo and bullfrogs.

I sat in the hall and waited. While I waited, I heard Elizabeth in Emily's room. "Rise and shine," she said. "Busy day."

Boy, are the weekdays busy at the big house. Daddy hurries to his office downstairs (he works at home now). Elizabeth hurries off to her office. Sam and Charlie rush to the high school, Kristy catches the bus for the middle school, David Michael catches the bus for Stoneybrook Elementary, I catch the bus for Stoneybrook Academy, and Andrew's carpool picks him up to go to his preschool. Busy, busy, busy.

"Okay, Emily," I heard Elizabeth say. "Put on your bathrobe."

"No!"

"Come on."

"No! No, no, no!"

Hmm.

At breakfast, Emily would not sit in her high chair. "No!" she shrieked. She kicked her feet. She kicked so hard she knocked a carton of orange juice off the table.

"*Now* do you see what I mean?" David Michael said to me.

I nodded, wide-eyed. "Yeah."

Daddy set Emily on the floor, away from the spilled orange juice. "Emily," he said patiently. "No kicking."

Emily lay down. She banged her fists on the tiles.

"Calm down, Emily," said Daddy.

"No, *no*, NO!"

Emily yelled so loudly she hurt my ears. "I better go," I said. "I do not want to be late." I flew out the door to meet Hannie.

Well, for heaven's sake. David Michael was right after all. Emily Michelle had turned into a little monster.

Stoneybrook Academy

"Karen! You are all out of breath," said Hannie.

"I ran here really fast," I replied. I was standing at the bus stop with my big-house best friend. "I could not wait to get out of my house. Emily is a monster," I said. "Shh. Listen — I bet you can hear her screaming all the way over here."

Hannie and I stopped talking. We could not hear Emily. But Hannie wanted me to tell her what had happened. So I did. When we reached school, I had to tell the story again, to Nancy.

"She had a *temper* tantrum," I finished up, as my friends and I walked into our classroom.

"Boy," said Nancy, "I sure hope Danny never has temper tantrums." (Danny is Nancy's baby brother.)

Hannie and Nancy and I put our things in our cubbies. Then we sat at our desks. Hannie and Nancy get to sit next to each other in the back row. I have to sit in the front row. That is because I am a glasses-wearer. I sit right in front of Ms. Colman's desk. Guess what. Ms. Colman is a glasses-wearer, too. So are Natalie Springer and Ricky Torres. They sit on either side of me. (Ricky is my pretend husband.)

The other kids in my class trickled into the room. I saw Pamela, Leslie, and Jannie. (They are sort of like the Three Musketeers, only not very nice.) I saw the boys — Bobby, who used to be a bully, and Hank and Chris and Omar and Ian. Then came

Sara Ford. Addie Sidney rolled through the door in her wheelchair. The last to arrive were the twins, Tammy and Terri Barkan, and Audrey Green. Eighteen kids in all. Plus Ms. Colman.

"Good morning, girls and boys," said our teacher.

Ms. Colman took roll. And then . . . she made a Surprising Announcement. I just love Surprising Announcements.

"Class, you have been working hard this fall," she said. "I am very proud of you. You should be proud of yourselves, too. And so should your families. I thought the people in your families might like to see what you have been working on. It is time for you to show off a little. So I have decided that we will have an autumn program for our families. It will be called 'Fall Is . . .' We will hold it at the end of next week. We will display some of your classwork, and we will make refreshments to serve to our guests. Also, we will read aloud the fall stories we will be writing."

Yes! Excellent! This sounded like gigundo fun. I just love showing off my work. And I like having an audience. I could not wait to read my story to everybody.

I turned around to grin at my friends in the back of the room. Hannie smiled back at me. But Nancy did not. She did not look happy.

Nancy raised her hand.

"Yes?" said Ms. Colman.

"Does everyone *have* to read their stories out loud?' asked Nancy.

"Yes," replied Ms. Colman. "That will be part of the program."

"Oh." Nancy slumped in her seat.

I faced the front of the room again. I thought about a fall story I could write. I wondered what kinds of refreshments we would make. I counted the days until our "Fall Is . . ." program. Eleven. How could I possibly wait eleven days for something so wonderful?

Nancy's Problem

At lunchtime that day, Nancy was very quiet. She barely spoke to Hannie and me. She just ate her sandwich and her banana. She did not even laugh when Hannie accidentally made milk squirt out of her nose. She just chewed and swallowed, chewed and swallowed.

On the playground I said, "Who wants to play hopscotch?"

"Me!" cried Hannie.

"You want to?" I asked Nancy.

She shook her head.

"How about jumping rope?"

"Nope."

"Jacks, then."

"Nope."

"Nancy, what is the matter?" Hannie finally asked.

Nancy shrugged.

"Come on," I said. "Tell us."

Nancy looked at the ground. "I do not wannareemyf . . ." she mumbled.

"What?" said Hannie and I.

"I do not want to read my fall story by myself in front of all those parents and guests at our program," said Nancy.

"Why not?" asked Hannie.

"I will be too scared."

"But everyone else will have to read their stories," I pointed out. "You will not be alone."

"That does not matter," said Nancy. "I do not care."

"We can help you practice," suggested Hannie.

"Yeah. That is a great idea," I agreed. "We will help you."

Nancy still did not look very happy.

"I know!" I said. "I have another idea. Come on. Let's find Ms. Colman."

Even though recess was not over, Nancy and Hannie and I ran inside Stoneybrook Academy. Then we walked to our classroom (since you are not supposed to run in the halls). Ms. Colman was sitting at her desk.

"Hello, girls," she said. "Is anything wrong?"

"We need to talk to you," I replied. "Nancy does not want to read her story at the fall program."

"She is scared," added Hannie.

"I see," said Ms. Colman. "What are you scared of, Nancy?"

"I am scared of reading in front of so many people."

"I imagine that some of the other kids might feel a little scared, too," said Ms.

Colman. "But this will be a good experience for you. It is called public speaking. It is very important."

"Couldn't I just read my story to you?" asked Nancy. "Before the program? I could work really hard and finish it early. Or maybe I could read it to you and Hannie and Karen. That would be a group of people. And I think it would be a very good experience for me."

Ms. Colman smiled. "If you would like to practice in front of us, that would be fine. But then you must read your story during the program, along with everyone else."

Nancy sighed. "Okay," she said.

The Three Musketeers went outside again to finish up recess.

"We really will help you, Nancy," I said as we waited to play tetherball. "You can count on us."

"Right," said Hannie.

"Okay," said Nancy again. She had not smiled once all morning.

Charlie's Monster

After school that day, Hannie ran across the street to the big house. Then Mrs. Dawes drove Nancy to the big house. The Three Musketeers were going to work on Nancy's public speaking.

We sat in a row on the front steps.

"Okay," I said. "Why don't you try saying a song or a poem or something? Just a short one."

"And just for us," said Hannie.

"What should I say?" asked Nancy.

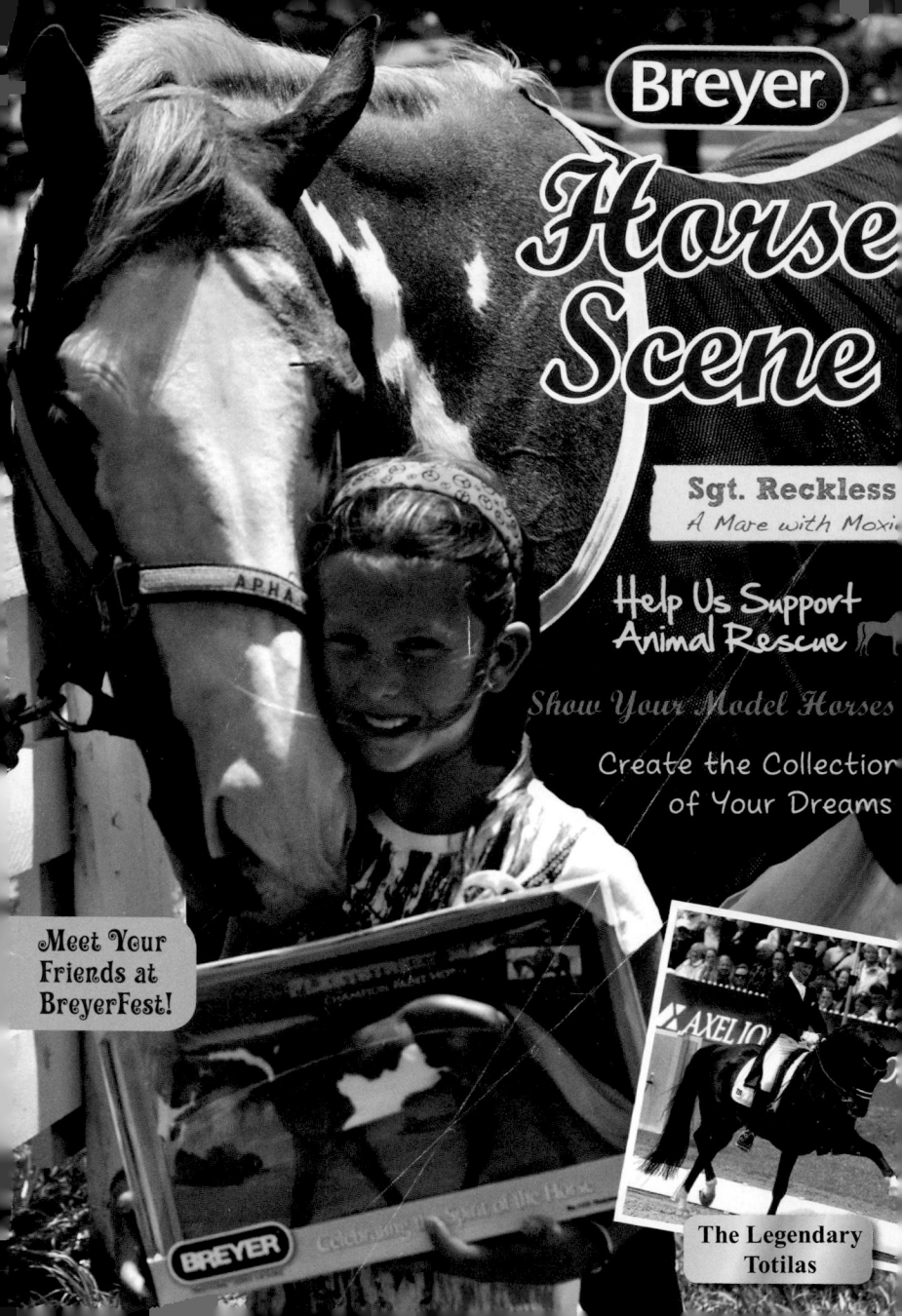

"Anything," replied Hannie. "How about 'Twinkle, Twinkle, Little Star'? Just say it. You do not have to sing it."

"Um, okay. Twinkletwinklelittlestarhowiwon — "

"Wait, wait! Slow down, Nancy," I said. "You are talking so fast I cannot understand you."

"Okay. Twinkle, twinkle, little . . ."

"Now I cannot hear you," said Hannie.

"Yeah, talk louder. Use a big outdoor voice," I said.

Nancy sighed. "I cannot even do this in front of my best friends. How will I ever do it for a whole audience?"

"You will be able to," said Hannie. "I just know it."

"How do you know?" asked Nancy.

"I don't know."

"You have done things like this before," I pointed out. "You have been in plays and things. You did not mind the audience then."

"Well, I do now," said Nancy. "I have

changed. I mind the audience. I mind it very much."

"Okay, pretend the audience is not there," said Hannie.

"Yeah," I agreed. "Try 'Twinkle, Twinkle' again and pretend Hannie and I are not here."

"Where are you?" asked Nancy.

"I don't know. We are just not here. Can you pretend that?"

"Maybe," said Nancy. "Okay. Twinkle, twinkle, little star . . . Well, this is stupid. How can I pretend you are not here when I am looking right at you?"

I sighed. "Let's stop for today," I said. "I think we have practiced enough. Are you ready to stop, Nancy?"

"Yes," she replied.

"Yes," added Hannie. She looked very relieved.

We called Mrs. Dawes and told her Nancy was ready to go home. After Mrs. Dawes had picked her up, Hannie left, too.

I kicked at the dry leaves in our front yard. I rustled through them. Then I heard noises coming from the garage. I heard hammering, and a scraping sound. I crept to the garage. The side door was partly open, so I peered inside. I found myself looking at . . . a monster. "Aughhhh!" I screamed. "A monster!"

"Karen!" It was Charlie's voice. "You scared me!"

"*I* scared *you*?" I leaned further into the garage. Then I saw that the monster was not really a monster. At least, not yet. It was the monster Charlie was making for the parade. And it was only half finished. But it was already very scary. Charlie had made the monster's body out of chicken wire. He had tried some clothes on it to see how they looked. On the floor around the monster were more clothes, a wig, an awful-looking mask, a hammer, some wires, and lots of tools.

Charlie was gazing proudly at the monster. "You know what?" he said. "I think I will make the monster's eyes out of blinking red lights. How does that sound?"

"It sounds . . . scary," I said.

I shivered.

Please Come

The next morning, I got ready for school very carefully. I tried not to do anything that would upset Emily. At breakfast time I gave her a special chocolate candy I had been saving. Then I talked quietly to Emily and told her about our autumn program at school. "Doesn't that sound like fun?" I asked her.

"No!" Emily swept her hand across the tray of her high chair. Everything on the tray crashed to the floor.

"I didn't do it!" I cried. Then I ran upstairs to brush my teeth.

I could hear Emily shrieking in the kitchen. I heard something else crash. By the time I went downstairs again, Emily was lying in the hallway by the front door. She was kicking her legs and pounding her fists into the rug.

Kristy and Sam and Charlie and David Michael and Andrew and I stepped around her and over her. Then we hurried out the door and off to our schools. My noisy bus seemed peaceful compared to Emily. "Whew," I said as Hannie and I found seats.

In school that morning, Ms. Colman said, "Class, today we must begin planning our fall program." (Goody, I thought.) "We need to do several things. We need to make invitations. We will do that today, so you can take them home with you. We also need to talk about the refreshments we will make, and about which of your classwork to display. Let's start with the projects we have been working on. Which things should we show off to your families?"

I shot my hand in the air. "Our autumn leaf pictures," I said.

Omar raised his hand. "How about the autumn spelling tests?"

Ms. Colman smiled. "Oh! Good idea. The special tests."

The tests Omar and Ms. Colman were talking about really were special. They were special because my classmates and I had studied our autumn words very hard, and every single one of us had gotten 100%. Ms. Colman had put a smiling pumpkin sticker at the top of each paper.

My friends and I talked some more. We decided to put our autumn leaf pictures and our spelling tests on the bulletin board. We decided to display our science projects on tables in the back of the room.

"All right. Now what about refreshments?" asked Ms. Colman.

"Cookies and punch!" called Pamela Harding.

"That is fine," replied Ms. Colman. "But maybe we can make refreshments that would remind us of autumn."

"Apple cider?" suggested Ian.

"Great," said Ms. Colman.

"How about cookies in the shapes of pumpkins and leaves?" said Hannie.

"Fantastic," said Ms. Colman.

When we had finished planning our refreshments, Ms. Colman turned to the chalkboard. "Boys and girls," she said, "let's think about our invitations now. What do we need to say on them?"

"That we are going to have a program," said Bobby.

"And we want our families to come to it," added Natalie.

"Is that all?" asked Ms. Colman.

"We better say when it is," said Addie.

"And where," said Hank.

Together we wrote our invitation. Ms.

Colman put the words on the board. Then we copied them onto orange paper. The outside of each invitation said, "Please come . . ." Inside was the rest of the information. I could not wait to bring my invitation home to my big-house family.

Frankenstone

Guess what. Emily Monster Michelle had a huge, noisy temper tantrum every single morning that week. When I went to bed on Friday night, I said to David Michael, "Emily better not ruin our weekend."

"Yeah. I want to sleep late tomorrow," he replied.

But Emily surprised us. She did not have a temper tantrum. She let David Michael sleep. And at breakfast she ate her food quite nicely. She did not say no once.

"Why is she being so good?" I whispered to Kristy.

Kristy raised one eyebrow. "I am not sure," she answered.

We decided to enjoy it.

"Who wants to see the monster?" Charlie asked then. "It is almost finished. I think I can finish it today."

"I do!" I cried.

"Me, too!" said Andrew.

"Me, me!" said Emily.

In the end, all my brothers and sisters said they wanted to see the monster. We waited on the driveway while Charlie brought it out of the garage. He leaned it against a tree. It was huge.

I took a good look at the monster. "Ooh, scary!" I said.

The monster was wearing a black coat, black pants, and heavy black workboots. Its face was greenish. On its head sat a mop of black hair. I could see two little pins at the sides of its neck. Spookiest of all, the monster's eyes did glow red, and they blinked on and off.

"It is a boy monster," said David Michael thoughtfully. "A he. And he really does look like Frankenstein."

"Thank you," replied Charlie. "But guess what. I gave him a new name. See if you can guess it. Here is a clue: He lives in Stoneybrook. Any guesses?"

"Big Scary Monster from Stoneybrook?" suggested Andrew.

Charlie smiled. "Well, no."

"I give up," David Michael and I said at the same time.

"Okay," said Charlie. "His name is Frankenstone."

"Frank for short," added Sam.

Kristy giggled. "Pretty funny!" she said. "I like that."

So did everyone else. Charlie looked very pleased with Frankenstone.

"What do you have to do to finish him?" asked Sam.

"Give him hands," replied Charlie. "And maybe fangs. And — I don't know — maybe see if I can figure out some way to make him move. Or some way to sound as if he's talking."

"Or groaning," I suggested.

"Oh, that's good," said Charlie. "Groaning. I like that."

Charlie spent hours working on the monster that day. By late in the afternoon, he decided Frank was finished. My brothers and sisters and I gathered to look at him again.

"Watch this," said Charlie. He stood behind Frankenstone. He fiddled with something on the monster's back.

Frankenstone's eyes lit up. Then he raised his arm. "Moooooahhhh-ha-ha!" he groaned. He lowered his arm. Then his head turned from side to side.

"Yikes," whispered Kristy. "That is really spooky."

"In a big way," I agreed.

Charlie grinned. "I am glad you like him."

Charlie and Sam lugged Frank into the garage.

I stared after them. All the little hairs on the back of my neck were standing on end.

The Big Scare

That night, Hannie and Nancy came to my house for a sleepover. They brought their sleeping bags. Daddy and Elizabeth let us eat supper in my bedroom. We had hamburgers and French fries and apple juice. For dessert we ate Popsicles.

"Yum," said Hannie when we had finished.

"Yum, yum," said Nancy. "What should we do now?"

"Talk about our Halloween costumes," I suggested.

"Halloween?" said Nancy. "Boy, I have not thought about my costume."

"I have," said Hannie. "I want to be a shepherd."

"A shepherd?" I repeated. "Really?"

"Well, maybe not."

"Good-bye, girls!" called Daddy then. "Elizabeth and I are leaving now."

"Okay!" I called back.

Nannie was going out that night, too. In fact, she had already left. So had Kristy. Charlie and Sam were in charge.

My friends and I talked about our costumes some more. We heard Sam put Emily Michelle to bed. We heard him go downstairs again. Then we heard the TV come on. Sam, Charlie, David Michael, and Andrew had planned to watch some movie together.

"Now what?" I asked my friends when we ran out of costume ideas.

"Let's turn out the lights and tell scary stories," said Hannie.

So we did. The only light we left on

was a flashlight. We passed it around to whoever was telling a story. After awhile, Nancy nudged me.

"Did you hear something?" she whispered.

The Three Musketeers stopped talking and listened.

"Karen!" a voice called.

"It is only David Michael," I said. I stood up and opened my door. I leaned into the hallway. "What?" I yelled.

"Can you guys come down here for a sec?" he asked.

"Okay!" I turned back to my friends. "Come on. I think he wants to show us something."

Hannie and Nancy and I ran downstairs. Guess what. Downstairs was all dark.

"What happened to the lights?" whispered Nancy.

"I don't know," I said. "And where is David Michael? Where are the boys?" We were standing in the front hallway. I fumbled around for the light switch. I could not find it. "David Michael?" I called.

No answer.

"Um, Karen, what is that?" asked Hannie in a shaky voice.

I turned and saw . . . two red lights. They were blinking in the dining room. "Aughhh!" I screamed. "It is the monster! Frankenstone has come to life!"

The lights were moving toward us. Slowly, very slowly. I could see Frank's head. I could see his arm going up and down.

"Moooooahhhh-ha-ha!" groaned Frank.

"Eeeeee! Yikes!" shrieked Hannie and Nancy. They grabbed my hands.

"Charlie!" I called. "Charlie! Where are you? You made a better monster than you thought! He is *alive!*"

"Run up the stairs!" yelled Hannie.

But just then the lights came on. I saw Frankenstone up close. Right behind him were Charlie, Sam, David Michael, and Andrew.

"Gotcha!" cried David Michael.

The boys had played a big joke on us.

Hannie and Nancy and I started to laugh then. But I had to admit something to myself.

I was a little afraid of Frankenstone.

I Pledge Allegiance

Nancy and Hannie and I had trouble falling asleep that night. We lay awake thinking about monsters and Dracula and Frankenstein and Frankenstone. But finally we did fall asleep. And the next thing I knew it was morning.

"Karen?" asked Nancy when we had eaten breakfast. "Hannie? Would you help me practice my public speaking again, please?"

"Sure," said Hannie.

"And I know just how to help you," I

added. "You need to practice in front of a real audience — just a small one. But not Hannie and me. You know you can mess up in front of us. So I think you do not try very hard. But you might try harder in front of a real audience."

"What real audience?" asked Nancy.

"Daddy, Elizabeth, Nannie, Kristy, Sam, Andrew, Emily, David Michael, and Charlie," I replied. I counted on my fingers. "Nine people. Plus Hannie and me. You can say something in front of them," I went on. "It will be easy. You know them. You like them."

"We-ell . . ." said Nancy.

"Come on," said Hannie. "You have to do it sometime. Besides, you were the one who said you wanted to practice."

"I know. But I did not mean in front of so many people."

"For heaven's sake! At our autumn program, you will have to speak in front of lots more —" I began to say. But Hannie kicked me.

"Let's just try it," she said loudly.

So I ran around and talked to everyone in my big-house family. They all said they would be glad to be an audience. Then Hannie and I helped Nancy choose something to say.

"It should be something you know really, really well," I said.

"How about the Pledge of Allegiance?" suggested Hannie.

"Okay," said Nancy. "Let me practice it in front of you guys first."

"But you have memorized the pledge," I said.

"I better practice it anyway," replied Nancy. "Are you ready? Okay. I pledge allegiance to the flag of the United States of America. And to the republic . . ."

Of course, Nancy knows the pledge perfectly. She did not say one word wrong. Plus, she spoke loudly and not too fast.

"Great!" I cried. "Okay. Now try it in front of your audience."

My big-house family had gathered in the

living room. Hannie sat down with them. Nancy and I stood in front of them.

"And now," I began, "I am pleased to present Nancy Dawes!"

Nancy stepped forward. I ran off to the side and sat next to Hannie. I smiled at Nancy. I wanted her to feel comfortable.

"I — I pledge," said Nancy. She was looking at her audience with big, frightened eyes. "I pledge," she said again. And then she burst into tears. She ran out of the living room.

Hannie and I ran after her. "Um, the show is over," I called to the audience. "Sorry."

Nancy was in my bedroom. She was crying. "See? I could not do it," she said. She sniffled loudly.

"Well — " I began to say.

"And if I could not say the Pledge of Allegiance in front of your family," Nancy rushed on, "how will I ever read my story to all the people at the program on Friday?"

"You *will* be able to do it," I said. "I know it. We will just have to keep working."

Frank Disappears

Emily had not had any tantrums on Saturday. She did not have any on Sunday. But on Monday morning . . .

"No! *No! NO!" Clunk. Slam. Crash.*

Emily had a huge tantrum. I escaped out the door and ran to the school bus. In the afternoon, I was in no hurry to go back inside my house. So after I hopped off the bus and called good-bye to Hannie, I stopped by our garage. I thought maybe I would take a peek at Frankenstone.

I pushed the door open. I peered inside.

I stared at Frank's corner. It looked empty. I stepped a bit closer. The corner *was* empty.

Frankenstone was gone.

I told myself not to panic. Maybe Charlie had put him in some other part of the garage after the big scare on Saturday night. I looked in every inch of the garage. No Frank.

That shiver ran down my spine again. Frank had escaped. He really had come to life!

I let out a huge scream. Then I flew outside. *Thud!* I had bumped into someone . . . or something. I screamed again.

"Karen! What on earth?" It was Charlie. He had just come home from school. "What is the matter?"

"Frank is gone!" I shrieked. "He came to life and escaped!"

"You mean he is missing?" exclaimed Charlie.

"Yes!" I was gasping for breath. I could hardly speak.

"Are you sure?"

"Go look."

Charlie barged into the garage. He turned on the light. He ran from corner to corner. He looked on things and in things and under things. Finally, he let out a sigh.

"We better call the police," I said. "They should know that a monster is on the loose. Who knows what he could do."

"Karen," said Charlie patiently, "Frank did not come to life. He is not on the loose. I think he was stolen. Come on. Help me look for clues. I have to find Frankenstone."

Karen Brewer, Private Eye

"**W**hy do you think Frank was stolen?" I asked Charlie.

"Because he is such a good monster," Charlie replied. "He is so good that I think someone else wanted him for one of the other floats."

"You mean like the kids on the basketball team?" I asked. "They stole Frank so they could have a good monster on their float?"

"Maybe," said Charlie. "Or anyone else could have done it. The kids in the school band, the kids in the glee club. There are an awful lot of teams and groups at SHS."

"Do you really want me to help you look for clues?" I asked. "I am very good at that. I am a good detective."

"Great," replied Charlie. "Then you may be my assistant private eye. You can help me catch the thief."

"Goody," I said.

"All right. Let's start here in the garage," began Charlie. "At the scene of the crime. Look for anything suspicious."

Charlie and I opened the doors so we could see better. At first all we saw was garage stuff — bicycles and a ladder and some old toys and cans of paint. I stepped outside. I looked at the driveway. I leaned over. I looked harder.

"Hey, Charlie!" I called. "Come here."

"What did you find, Karen?"

"This," I said, pointing to the driveway. "At first I thought it was just mud. But it looks like a tire track."

"Hmm. Very good clue," said Charlie. "Do you know why?"

"No. Why?"

"Because the only car here is mine, the Junk Bucket. Mom drove her car to work this morning, and the van is out being repaired. The Junk Bucket is parked in the street. It has been there all day. So this tire track must be from . . ."

"Someone else's car!" I finished.

"Right," said Charlie. "And probably from the car that belongs to the person who stole Frank." Charlie paused. "Which also means," he continued, "that whoever stole Frank must be old enough to drive. Let me see. The kids in freshman chorus could not have taken Frank. They are too young to drive. So are the kids in the Eighty-Eights. That is the piano players group. I wonder who else I can cross off the list of suspects."

Charlie went inside to find some paper and a pen. He wanted to make notes. I kept searching for clues. Just as I heard Charlie

return to the garage, I spotted something else.

"I think I found another clue!" I called.

Charlie trotted over to me. "What?" he asked.

"These little tiny holes. Here in the dirt. I do not know what they are. But they could be — "

"Hey, I think they are cleat marks!" cried Charlie. "You know who wears cleats? Football players and soccer players, that's who. We know Frank was not stolen by someone on the football team, of course. So I bet someone on the soccer team took him. Come on, Karen. Want to take a little ride over to Buddy Chester's house? He's the captain of the soccer team."

"Sure!" I said.

And before I knew it, Charlie and I were driving along in the Junk Bucket. But guess what. When we reached Buddy's house, his brother told us Buddy was not at home.

"He is in Deerfield with the soccer team.

They have an away game today," said Buddy's brother.

"Well," Charlie said to me as we were driving home, "I guess the soccer team did not steal Frank. They are all in Deerfield today. We will just have to keep searching for clues."

Fall Is Stinky

It was Thursday. Three days had gone by. Emily had had three more tantrums. But Charlie and I had not found any more clues to our mystery. We had no idea who had stolen the monster or where he was. Charlie was getting worried.

In school, Nancy was getting worried, too. That was because the fall program would be held the very next day. Soon she would have to read her story in front of an audience.

I was not worried, though. I was looking forward to reading my story. And I was having fun getting ready for the program. My classmates and I had lots of things to do. We were making apple cider. We were baking gingerbread. (That was Ms. Colman's idea.) We were cutting out cookies in fall shapes. Plus, we were putting the last touches on our bulletin board, and on the display of our science projects. And we were finishing our autumn stories.

Our classroom was a mess.

Ms. Colman had divided us into groups. Each group worked on one activity for awhile. Then we switched, and moved on to another activity. I was cutting out cookies. Hannie was making apple cider. Nancy was supposed to be working on her story. Most of us had finished writing our stories. Now we were just copying them neatly so we could read them easily the next day. But Nancy said she had decided she did not like her story anymore. She said she was going to start a new one.

"Hum, de-hum, de-hum." I hummed away while I cut out cookies. I cut out a pumpkin and a leaf and an apple. I looked at Nancy. Her head was bent over her paper. She was writing busily.

At lunchtime, Hannie and Nancy and I sat together in the cafeteria. We had bought chocolate milk and we were blowing bubbles in it.

When we stopped, I said, "Nancy? Did you finish your story?"

"Yup." She nodded. "And I brought it with me. Want to hear it?"

"Why did you bring it with you?" asked Hannie.

"You will see," replied Nancy. "Okay, listen. This is my new story." Nancy cleared her throat. Then she began to read. "Fall is stinky," she said. "I hate fall. In the fall, leaves fall down and they are stinky and you just have to rake them up. That is stinky, too. So — "

"Nancy?" Hannie interrupted. "I do not

think Ms. Colman is going to like that story very much."

Nancy smiled. "I know. That is what I think, too. So she will not let me read it tomorrow. I will not have to read after all."

I was thinking about what a good, sneaky plan that was, when Ms. Colman joined us at our table. "Nancy," she said, "I just realized that I have not read your new story yet. Where is it? Did you leave it in your desk? I would like to look at it."

"Um, well, it is right here," replied Nancy. Nancy handed her stinky fall story to our teacher.

Ms. Colman read it to herself. She frowned. Then she folded the paper and stuck it in her notebook. "You do know that you may not read that tomorrow, don't you?" Ms. Colman said to Nancy.

Nancy tried not to smile. "Yes," she replied.

"Good," said Ms. Colman. "I thought so. After recess, you are to begin a new story.

One that you may read tomorrow. I will expect it by the end of the day. If you do not finish it, I will give you a fall poem to read."

Well, for heaven's sake.

Ms. Colman was not exactly mad. She hardly ever gets mad. But she was not exactly happy, either.

Underwear

Nancy did write a new story that afternoon. It was almost the same as the first story she had written. It was a very nice story about an oak leaf named Linda that did not want to fall off of her tree, so she hung on until the first snow came. Linda got to play in the snow, and *then* she was ready to drop to the ground.

When Nancy gave it to Ms. Colman, our teacher smiled. "Thank you, Nancy," she said. "This is lovely."

After school, Nancy and Hannie came

over to the big house again. We had one last chance to help Nancy with her public speaking. Nancy brought her story with her. (Ms. Colman had made a photocopy of it so Nancy could practice.)

"All right," I said firmly when my friends and I were sitting in my room. "This is it, Nancy. Now or never. Read your story."

"And do not even *think* about the audience," added Hannie. "Do not look at us. Just look at your paper."

"Oh, wait! I have a better idea," I exclaimed. "Imagine that the people in the audience are wearing only their underwear."

"Their underwear?" Nancy began to giggle.

"What is so funny?" I asked.

"I am thinking of Bobby's underpants."

Hannie and I began to giggle, too.

"Hey, I know!" said Nancy. "Go get David Michael. I want to try reading my story while I think about his underwear."

I found David Michael and pulled him

into my room. Nancy took one look at him and started giggling again. She could not stop.

"Why is she laughing?" asked David Michael.

"Um, never mind," I replied. "You can go now."

I was glad to see Nancy laughing. But now she could not read her story because she was laughing too hard. Finally Hannie and I gave up. We just could not seem to help Nancy.

Mrs. Dawes picked Nancy up and drove her home. When she was gone, I said to Hannie, "I am a little worried about tomorrow. I thought Nancy would finally be able to read her story. Now I am not so sure. I wonder what is going to happen."

Hannie shrugged. She looked worried, too.

Hannie ran home then. I decided to search for clues to the monster mystery. I walked to the garage. I looked at the drive-way. I looked in the grass next to the driveway. Then I looked in the garage. While I was in the garage, I remembered something. I remembered that a year ago, at Halloween, Charlie had helped play a trick on another football team. The team was called the Bricktown Bulldogs. They beat Charlie's team almost every year. So, as a joke, Charlie stole their enormous stuffed bulldog. It was the Bulldogs' mascot. Charlie did not keep it. He just hid it until the big football game was over. Then he returned it. Charlie had hidden it in Daddy's toolshed. It was a very good hiding place. And it gave me a very good idea.

I ran inside the big house. "Hey, Charlie!" I called.

"Yeah?" Charlie was doing his homework.

"I thought of something. I know where you should look for Frank. You should look for him in toolsheds," I told him.

"In toolsheds? Why?"

"Because our shed was such a good hiding place for the bulldog. Remember?"

"The bulldog! Bricktown's bulldog," Charlie exclaimed. A grin spread across his face. Then he said, "Karen, you are a genius!"

The Return of Frank

"Why am I a genius?" I asked Charlie.

My big brother was rushing around downstairs. He found his car keys. He found his wallet. He put on his jacket. "I will explain later. Or I will explain now in the car, if you want to come with me," he said.

"Okay. I will come. Where are we going?"

"To Bricktown," said Charlie.

Charlie and I told Nannie where we were going. Then we leaped into the Junk

Bucket. When we had fastened our seatbelts and pulled into the street, Charlie said, "Now I will tell you what is going on. We are driving to Bricktown because that is where Ellis Wood lives."

"Who is Ellis Wood?" I asked.

"He is the captain of the Bricktown Bulldogs. And I think he has Frank."

"*He* does? But why? The Bricktown Bulldogs are not going to be in your school parade," I said.

"No. You are right. But after the parade, SHS is going to play a game against the Bulldogs."

"Oh," I said. And then, *"Oh!"* Suddenly I understood.

"Get it?" asked Charlie.

"Got it. The captain of the Bulldogs stole Frank because last year, before the big game, *you* stole their *bulldog*."

"Exactly," replied Charlie. "At least, I am pretty sure that is what happened. We will know soon."

Charlie drove and drove. Bricktown is almost half an hour from Stoneybrook. Outside, it was just starting to grow dark. Lots of cars were on the road. People were leaving their schools and offices and businesses and going home. It was a peaceful time of day. But I felt excited.

"Okay," said Charlie after awhile. "Here we are in Bricktown. And I think this is Ellis's neighborhood. I hope I remember which is his hou— Oh, here it is. I think. Does that mailbox say 'Wood,' Karen?" Charlie had slowed the Junk Bucket down.

I peered out the window. "Yup."

Charlie turned the car around. He parked across the street from Ellis's house. We sat in the Junk Bucket and stared outside. I felt like a spy in a movie.

In Ellis's front yard were four guys. They were about Charlie's age. "Do you know them?" I whispered.

"I think they are all on the football team," Charlie answered.

We did not know what to do then, so we just sat and spied some more. Finally Ellis walked across the lawn to his garage. The other boys followed him. Ellis opened the garage door. He and the boys climbed into a car. Then they drove away. They left the garage door open behind them. They left the light on, too. And inside, propped against a lawnmower, Charlie and I saw . . .

"Frankenstone!" I yelped.

Charlie grinned at me. "Okay, Karen. I am going to make a run for it," he said. "You stay right here. I am going to lock you in the car. Then I will run to the garage and grab Frank. Unlock the door for me when I get back. Do it fast, okay?"

"Okay," I whispered.

I watched Charlie dash across the street and into the garage, and grab Frank. As he was running back to me, I pressed the Unlock button. Then Charlie tossed Frank into the backseat, and we drove off.

"We made it!" I cried.

"Thanks to you," replied Charlie. "You are a super detective, Karen."

Charlie was so happy that later, when Frank was safely back at the big house, he promised Andrew, Emily, David Michael, and me that we could ride on the float in the Halloween parade with him.

"I will get a monster costume for each of you," he said.

Yes!

Fall Is . . .

"No, no, no, no, no, *no*, NO!"

Emily was having her morning tantrum. She was making me nervous.

"That is not fair," I complained to David Michael. "Today is the day of our autumn program. If Emily makes me nervous and I mess up when I read my story, it will be all her fault."

"I hope she does not have a tantrum *while* you are reading your story," said David Michael. "That would be awful."

Oh, boy. I had not even thought about

that. Daddy and Nannie and Emily Michelle were going to come to "Fall Is . . ." What if Emily *did* have a tantrum, and right in the middle of my story? What if she had one during Nancy's story? That would be even worse.

I worried about Emily while I rode on the school bus. I worried during the morning at school. I worried during lunch and recess. Then, after recess, our guests began to arrive for the program. And I stopped worrying. When Emily walked through our doorway, holding Daddy's hand, she was grinning from ear to ear.

"Thank goodness," I whispered to Hannie.

When the mommies and daddies and grandparents and brothers and sisters and friends entered our room, they looked at the autumn decorations we had made. They looked at our leaf pictures and our science projects. They ate our refreshments. My friends and I tasted the refreshments, too. Our cookies were gigundoly good.

I showed Emily around the room by myself. "See?" I said. "I made that picture." I lifted her up so she could see it. "And that is my science project. When you are older, you will know about sea creatures, too. And over here is my cubby, and this is my desk."

Emily was happily looking through my desk when Ms. Colman said, "Attention, guests! It is time for our special presentation. Today my hard-working students will read their autumn stories to you. Please find seats at the back of the room. And will my students please stand over there at the side of the room."

In just a few minutes, the stories began. Ms. Colman asked Hannie to read first. Hannie proudly read her story about pumpkins. Then she smiled at the audience and returned to the side of the room. Omar read next. Then Natalie. Then Addie.

And then it was my turn. I carried my story to the front of the room. I felt just a teeny bit nervous. I *love* having an audience. But that does not mean I never feel nervous. I took a deep breath. That helped the butterflies in my tummy. Then I began to read.

When I finished, Emily clapped her hands. She had not had a tantrum. I grinned at her.

"Now," said Ms. Colman, "Nancy Dawes will read 'Linda Leaf's Snow Day.' Nancy? Please come to the front of the room."

Nancy turned to me with big scared eyes. "I cannot read my story with all these people looking at me," she whispered.

Oh. So *that* was the problem. Well, I knew just how to fix it.

I cleared my throat. "Ahem." Then I said, "Excuse me, everybody. Before Nancy reads her story, could you please turn your backs?"

Our audience looked surprised. So did Ms. Colman and my classmates. But every-

one turned around. Nancy glanced at me. I nodded to her. Then I turned my back, too.

"Linda Leaf was very sad," Nancy began. And then she read her entire story. She read loudly. She did not read too fast. When she finished, everyone clapped.

Nancy ran to me. "I did it!" she whispered.

Emily Disappears

Our autumn program was almost over. My classmates and I had finished reading our stories. Our guests were wandering around and eating again. I was showing Daddy my project on the sea creatures when Nannie rushed across the room to us.

"Where is Emily?" she asked. "Have you seen her?"

"I thought she was with you," said Daddy.

"*I* thought she was with *you*," said Nannie.

"Well, she must be right here some-where." Daddy looked around the room. Then he glanced into the hallway. "Hmm," he said.

We searched high and low in Ms. Colman's room, in case Emily was hiding.

"Is anything wrong?" asked Ms. Colman.

"We cannot find Emily," I told her.

Soon everyone was looking for Emily. Ms. Colman was looking for her, my classmates were looking for her, even our guests were looking for her.

Emily was not in the room. The searchers looked in the halls. They looked in the cafeteria and the gym. Then they began to look in the other classrooms.

Daddy ran from room to room. (He hardly ever runs.) Nannie's eyes filled with tears. "Don't worry, Nannie," I said. "We will find Emily. I know we will." I turned to Hannie and Nancy. "Come on, you guys. Let's go look on the playground."

On the way to the playground, we passed the kindergarten rooms. I saw Mr.

Posner, one of the teachers, and I waved to him. "Mr. Posner, have you seen my little sister? She is lost," I said.

Just then, a voice cried, "Hi! Look! Look at me!" The voice sounded like Emily's, and it had come from the back of Mr. Posner's room. I peered into the Imagination Corner.

There was Emily. She was wearing a straw hat and a tool belt, and she was grinning from ear to ear. "Come pay!" she called to me.

"Emily! We have been looking all over for you! You scared us!" I said. "Hey, Hannie, Nancy. Will you guys please find Daddy and Nannie, and tell them where Emily is?"

My friends ran off. A few minutes later, everyone stopped searching for Emily. Daddy and Nannie rushed into Mr. Posner's room. They hugged Emily. Nannie cried a little.

"Do not ever do that again!" exclaimed Daddy.

"We did not know where you were," added Nannie. "You must not run off like that."

"Okay," said Emily. She was still grinning.

"I guess Emily had been here for a few minutes before Karen saw her," said Mr. Posner. "I was busy with the children working at the math table, so I did not see her come in. She gets along very nicely with other children," he went on. "She is very cooperative."

"And happy," I said, looking at Emily's smile. "I think she really likes school. Do you like school, Emily?"

"Cool!" she cried.

I did not know whether that meant "cool" or "school," but it did not matter. Either way, she sounded excited. Suddenly, I understood something. Daddy and Nannie understood it then, too.

"Emily wants to go to school," I said.

This was why Emily had tantrums on

weekday mornings. She was the only kid at the big house who did not get to go to school. She did not like being left behind.

"Well, I think we can do something about that," said Daddy.

Emily's School

When we returned to the big house that afternoon, Daddy and Nannie went right to work. They wanted to find a preschool for Emily. Do you know what happened? They could not find one. Part of the reason was that Emily is only two. Most of the programs they found were for kids who are three or four. The rest of the reason was that school had already started. It was almost the end of October. The programs they did find for two-year-olds were full already.

At dinner that night, my family talked things over. Finally Kristy said, "What about starting a play group for Emily?"

"What is a play group?" asked David Michael.

"It is a group of children who get together a few times a week. They paint and play games and build with blocks and listen to stories. Only they do not go to a school. They move around from house to house. Mom, I bet we could start a play group for Emily, Sari Papadakis, and a few other little kids on the street. The group would be held here one day, at Sari's the next day, and so forth. Just for a couple of hours each time. That is long enough for a two-year-old."

"Kristy, that is a wonderful idea!" exclaimed Elizabeth.

"Fantastic," agreed Daddy.

"The best," said Nannie.

"Emily, you are going to go to school," I said. "*Emily's* school. A school just for you."

"Well, now, let's not get her hopes up," said Daddy. "We have not arranged this yet. We have not even talked to the Papadakises."

But guess what. In just two days, Emily's "school" was ready to go. Sari Papadakis would be part of it, and so would two other two-year-olds who live nearby — Petey Crosby and Nelson Rice.

Emily's first day of school was on Monday. The play group was going to be held at Sari's.

When I woke up on Monday morning, I bounced into Emily's room. "Good morning, Emily!" I cried. "Today is Monday, a school day. And *you* are going to school. You are a big girl."

"Cool?" Emily repeated. She climbed out of her bed.

"Yup. School. So come on. Time to get ready. What do you want to wear on your first day of school?"

Emily pulled open one of her bureau

drawers. "Socks?" she suggested.

"That is a good start," I said.

I helped Emily get dressed. Then I led her downstairs to the kitchen. Elizabeth put Emily in her high chair. I watched my little sister closely. I was waiting for her to throw a tantrum.

But she did not. She knew she was going to school like the rest of us kids. So she behaved herself. She ate her breakfast. When she was finished, she said, "All done."

Daddy took her out of her high chair. He wiped her face and hands. "Are you ready to go to school, Emily?" he asked.

"Ready," replied Emily.

So Daddy walked Emily across the street to Sari's house.

When I returned home from school that day, I found Emily sitting outside on the front steps with Nannie. "How was school?" I asked her.

"Cool! Pay! Make painting!" cried Emily.

She tugged at my sleeve. Then she pulled me inside to show me a painting that Nannie had taped to the refrigerator. "I big girl now," announced Emily.

My little sister was just a sister again. She was no longer a monster.

Four Little Monsters

One Saturday morning I woke up in my bed at the big house. I lay there with my fingers crossed. I was crossing them because I hoped that when I peeked out the window I would find sunshine. Rain would be a very, very bad thing. Why? Because today was the day of the SHS Halloween parade.

With my fingers still crossed (all of them), I sat up. I peered behind the window shade. I saw sunshine.

"Yes!" I cried.

I uncrossed my fingers. Then I threw on some clothes and ran downstairs. "Charlie! Charlie!" I called.

"In the kitchen, Karen," he replied.

I ran to the kitchen. "Okay, where is it?" I asked.

Charlie grinned at me. "What? You mean your costume? Gosh, I don't know. I hope I have not lost it."

I knew Charlie was teasing me. He had gotten together monster costumes for Emily, Andrew, David Michael, and me, just as he had promised. But he would not show them to us. "I will surprise you on the day of the parade," he kept saying.

Well, now it was the day of the parade. "Come on, Charlie. You know where my costume is. *Please* go get it," I begged him. "Get all of them. We cannot wait to see them."

That was true. By then, Emily, David Michael, and Andrew were with me. We were dying to see the costumes. We were hoping for fangs.

Charlie disappeared upstairs. When he returned to us, his arms were full. He handed out the parts of our costumes.

"Cool! A wart!" cried Andrew.

"Very realistic fangs," said David Michael.

"Oh, goody. Warty hands," I said.

"Hair!" exclaimed Emily. (Charlie had given her a fright wig.)

Charlie helped the four of us put on our costumes. When we had finished, he nodded his head. "Excellent monsters," he said. Then he called the rest of our family to look at us.

Kristy pretended she did not recognize us. "Aughh! Monsters!" she shrieked. She ran out of the room.

Soon it was time to drive to the high school. Charlie loaded Frankenstone into the Junk Bucket. David Michael and Andrew and I climbed in, too. Everyone else rode in the van. We met at SHS.

"Whoa. Look at all these people," I said to David Michael.

A huge crowd had gathered near the

football field. The floats were lining up for the parade. High school kids were setting things up on the floats, climbing onto the floats, unrolling banners, and putting on their costumes. Bustle, bustle, bustle.

Charlie led my brothers and sister and me to the football team's float. (Sam left to find the math club's float. He was going to ride on it dressed like an enormous number 5. He said he felt like a dork.)

"Hey, everybody! Here is Frank!" Charlie announced when he reached the float. "And here are our four little monsters."

Charlie helped us monsters onto the float. I looked around. I was going to be riding with Frankenstone, a mummy, Bigfoot, Dracula, a swamp creature, my brothers, and Emily. Cool.

I waited for the parade to start. (I was not very patient.) When it did, we rolled onto the street. We moved slowly past the high school. Then we headed downtown.

I looked out at the people watching the

parade. They were waving and calling to us.

"Happy Halloween, everybody!" I cried. "Happy Halloween from the little monsters!"

About the Author

ANN M. MARTIN lives in New York City and loves animals, especially cats. She has two cats of her own, Mouse and Rosie.

Other books by Ann M. Martin that you might enjoy are *Stage Fright*; *Me and Katie (the Pest)*; and the books in *The Baby-sitters Club* series.

Ann likes ice cream and *I Love Lucy*. And she has her own little sister, whose name is Jane.

Little Sister

Don't miss #67

KAREN'S TURKEY DAY

"Oh, my. Thanksgiving is only a day and a half away. There is not much left to buy," said Granny. "Let's see if we can find those cranberries."

The cranberries were completely sold out. Boo.

"We better hurry and get our turkey," I said. "We do not want anyone else to buy the last one."

I raced to the meat department. Granny had to run to keep up with me. There was not a single turkey in sight.

We looked everywhere. Finally Granny found two tiny ones buried under some packages of chicken wings.

"We cannot buy these turkeys. They do not look fresh at all," said Granny.

"Then what will we eat?" I asked.

LITTLE APPLE®

BABY-SITTERS

Little Sister™
by Ann M. Martin, author of *The Baby-sitters Club*®

☐ MQ44300-3	#1	Karen's Witch	$2.95
☐ MQ44259-7	#2	Karen's Roller Skates	$2.95
☐ MQ44299-7	#3	Karen's Worst Day	$2.95
☐ MQ44264-3	#4	Karen's Kittycat Club	$2.95
☐ MQ44258-9	#5	Karen's School Picture	$2.95
☐ MQ44298-8	#6	Karen's Little Sister	$2.95
☐ MQ44257-0	#7	Karen's Birthday	$2.95
☐ MQ42670-2	#8	Karen's Haircut	$2.95
☐ MQ43652-X	#9	Karen's Sleepover	$2.95
☐ MQ43651-1	#10	Karen's Grandmothers	$2.95
☐ MQ43650-3	#11	Karen's Prize	$2.95
☐ MQ43649-X	#12	Karen's Ghost	$2.95
☐ MQ43648-1	#13	Karen's Surprise	$2.95
☐ MQ43646-5	#14	Karen's New Year	$2.95
☐ MQ43645-7	#15	Karen's in Love	$2.95
☐ MQ43644-9	#16	Karen's Goldfish	$2.95
☐ MQ43643-0	#17	Karen's Brothers	$2.95
☐ MQ43642-2	#18	Karen's Home Run	$2.95
☐ MQ43641-4	#19	Karen's Good-Bye	$2.95
☐ MQ44823-4	#20	Karen's Carnival	$2.95
☐ MQ44824-2	#21	Karen's New Teacher	$2.95
☐ MQ44833-1	#22	Karen's Little Witch	$2.95
☐ MQ44832-3	#23	Karen's Doll	$2.95
☐ MQ44850-5	#24	Karen's School Trip	$2.95
☐ MQ44831-5	#25	Karen's Pen Pal	$2.95
☐ MQ44830-7	#26	Karen's Ducklings	$2.75
☐ MQ44829-3	#27	Karen's Big Joke	$2.95
☐ MQ44828-5	#28	Karen's Tea Party	$2.95
☐ MQ44825-0	#29	Karen's Cartwheel	$2.75
☐ MQ45645-8	#30	Karen's Kittens	$2.95
☐ MQ45646-6	#31	Karen's Bully	$2.95
☐ MQ45647-4	#32	Karen's Pumpkin Patch	$2.95
☐ MQ45648-2	#33	Karen's Secret	$2.95
☐ MQ45650-4	#34	Karen's Snow Day	$2.95
☐ MQ45652-0	#35	Karen's Doll Hospital	$2.95
☐ MQ45651-2	#36	Karen's New Friend	$2.95
☐ MQ45653-9	#37	Karen's Tuba	$2.95
☐ MQ45655-5	#38	Karen's Big Lie	$2.95
☐ MQ45654-7	#39	Karen's Wedding	$2.95
☐ MQ47040-X	#40	Karen's Newspaper	$2.95

More Titles... ▶

The Baby-sitters Little Sister titles continued...

☐ MQ47041-8	#41	Karen's School	$2.95
☐ MQ47042-6	#42	Karen's Pizza Party	$2.95
☐ MQ46912-6	#43	Karen's Toothache	$2.95
☐ MQ47043-4	#44	Karen's Big Weekend	$2.95
☐ MQ47044-2	#45	Karen's Twin	$2.95
☐ MQ47045-0	#46	Karen's Baby-sitter	$2.95
☐ MQ46913-4	#47	Karen's Kite	$2.95
☐ MQ47046-9	#48	Karen's Two Families	$2.95
☐ MQ47047-7	#49	Karen's Stepmother	$2.95
☐ MQ47048-5	#50	Karen's Lucky Penny	$2.95
☐ MQ48229-7	#51	Karen's Big Top	$2.95
☐ MQ48299-8	#52	Karen's Mermaid	$2.95
☐ MQ48300-5	#53	Karen's School Bus	$2.95
☐ MQ48301-3	#54	Karen's Candy	$2.95
☐ MQ48230-0	#55	Karen's Magician	$2.95
☐ MQ48302-1	#56	Karen's Ice Skates	$2.95
☐ MQ48303-X	#57	Karen's School Mystery	$2.95
☐ MQ48304-8	#58	Karen's Ski Trip	$2.95
☐ MQ48231-9	#59	Karen's Leprechaun	$2.95
☐ MQ48305-6	#60	Karen's Pony	$2.95
☐ MQ48306-4	#61	Karen's Tattletale	$2.95
☐ MQ48307-2	#62	Karen's New Bike	$2.95
☐ MQ25996-2	#63	Karen's Movie	$2.95
☐ MQ25997-0	#64	Karen's Lemonade Stand	$2.95
☐ MQ25998-9	#65	Karen's Toys	$2.95
☐ MQ26279-3	#66	Karen's Monsters	$2.95
☐ MQ43647-3		Karen's Wish Super Special #1	$3.25
☐ MQ44834-X		Karen's Plane Trip Super Special #2	$3.25
☐ MQ44827-7		Karen's Mystery Super Special #3	$3.25
☐ MQ45644-X		Karen's Three Musketeers Super Special #4	$2.95
☐ MQ45649-0		Karen's Baby Super Special #5	$3.25
☐ MQ46911-8		Karen's Campout Super Special #6	$3.25

Available wherever you buy books, or use this order form.

- -

Scholastic Inc., P.O. Box 7502, 2931 E. McCarty Street, Jefferson City, MO 65102

Please send me the books I have checked above. I am enclosing $_____
(please add $2.00 to cover shipping and handling). Send check or money order - no cash or C.O.D.s please.

Name_____ Birthdate_____

Address _____

City_____ State/Zip _____

Please allow four to six weeks for delivery. Offer good in U.S.A. only. Sorry, mail orders are not available to residents to Canada. Prices subject to change.

BLS495